This Twinkl Original
book belongs to:

_____

_____

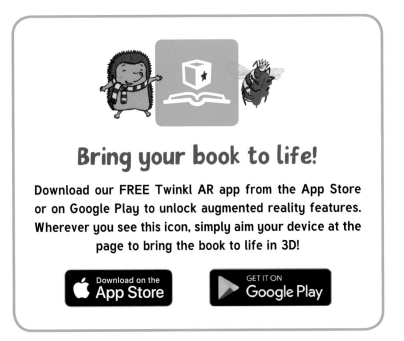

Bring your book to life!

Download our FREE Twinkl AR app from the App Store or on Google Play to unlock augmented reality features. Wherever you see this icon, simply aim your device at the page to bring the book to life in 3D!

First published 2018 by Twinkl Ltd.
197 Ecclesall Road, Sheffield S11 8HW

ISBN: 978-1-9997835-6-3

FSC
www.fsc.org

MIX
Paper from responsible sources
FSC® C022913

We're passionate about giving our children a sustainable future, which is why this book is made from Forest Stewardship Council® certified paper. Learn how our Twinkl Green policy gives the planet a helping hand at www.twinkl.com/twinkl-green.

Printed in the United Kingdom.

10 9 8 7 6 5 4 3 2 1

A catalogue record for this book is available from the British Library.

A Twinkl Original

Don't Hog the Hedge!

Twinkl Educational Publishing

"Goodness me!" snorted Hattie the Hedgehog. "It's half past September already. I haven't got time to play! I must finish my hibernation checklist."

Water
Bedding ✓
Toilet area
Alarm clock

As the leaves grew crispier, and the air colder,
Hattie worked hard to prepare her winter home.

She snuggled tightly into her cosy and comfortable
hedge, just in time for the Big Sleep.

SNACKS

TOILET →

Just as she was drifting off, little footsteps caused her to open her eyes.

"Who could that be?" she grumbled, as she stuck her furry and slightly damp nose out of the hedge.

Three dormice, Dylan, Dexter and Doris, popped up out of a patch of fallen leaves.

"We were just admiring the beautiful home you have made," Dylan squeaked. "Could we stay here for the Big Sleep too?"

"Your nest looks so wonderfully warm and you have prepared it so well. So, please...

don't hog the hedge!"

"Well, my hedge is only really set up for one," Hattie grunted. "But as you're all only little, I can probably find some space for you, just this once."

Just as soon as they had settled in, Hattie heard a new, very strange sound heading their way.

Thud...

shuffle...

shuffle...

Thud!

Toby the Toad came to a stop
in front of the hedge.

"Hello! Can I hunker down in that
marvellous hedge of yours?" he
croaked loudly.

"Your nest looks so comfy and you have prepared it so well. So, please...

don't hog the hedge!"

"You really should have sorted out a place to stay sooner!" Hattie scolded. "But I suppose you can stay if you promise not to leap around too much."

Hattie budged up closer to the dormice to give Toby more room. The hedge was very short of space but it was much cosier than before.

"Thank you so much for sharing with us," Doris said.

"You're my hero!" Toby declared.

As the animals thanked her, Hattie's prickly mood began to change.

"I've never been called a hero before!" she said proudly.

She happily snuggled down tight into her leafy bed with her new companions, but just as her tired little eyes gently closed...

Buzzzzzzzzzz! A bumblebee appeared.

"Sorry to disturb you all," she called, "but
I can see that the home you have made is,
quite simply, fit for a queen. And well, here
I am – Queen Beatrice!"

"Your nest looks so safe and you have prepared it so well. So, please...

don't hog the..."

"Yeah, yeah, yeah! You don't need to ask,
Your Majesty," Hattie chuckled. "Just come
on in and make yourself at home."

What a squashed-up bunch they were! Hattie's spikes tickled Toby's toes and everyone was trying hard to avoid Queen Beatrice's sting.

Eventually, they all settled down but then...

Sob... sniffle... sob...

"Waaah!"

Billy, a young and very upset bat, floated gently
down beside the hedge.

"I'm lost! I can't find my family," he sobbed. "Can
I hang out in your company for a little while?"

Hattie looked around at her cramped little shelter.

"I don't think there's any hedge left to hog!" she said. "We simply cannot all fit in."

But then, she did something totally unexpected...

"You can have my space," Hattie offered.

She stepped out of the hedge to make room for the lost little bat.

But then, her friends did something even more unexpected...

They all stepped out
of the hedge as well!

"This hedge is not a home without
you, Hattie," squeaked Dexter. "Let's
find a place where we can all fit."

Hattie felt warm and fuzzy inside, even though it was freezing outside!

So, they set off and soon found a new, more perfect spot for their big and well-deserved sleep...

...and they found Billy's family there too.

All of them!

Continue the learning with exclusive teacher-created resources to support you in the classroom. There's also an eBook, a PowerPoint, and much more!

Visit twinkl.com/**originals**